W9-CAT-218

Copyright © 2006 by Sue Grundfest

Love Dog Adventures LLC
New York, NY

All rights reserved. No part of this book may be reproduced or transmitted
in any form or by any electronic or mechanical means, including photocopying
and information storage and retrieval systems, without permission in writing
from the publisher, except by a reviewer, who may quote brief passages.

ISBN 13: 978-0-9776150-0-1
ISBN 10: 0-9776150-0-6

Printed in the United States of America

10 9 8 7 6 5 4 3 2 1

For Coco,
Whose love has no boundaries,
and for all those whose lives she has touched

COCO

THE LO♥E DOG

Loves

_____

My Story
by Coco the Love Dog

"Most dogs like to sit in the sun or chase a ball all day, but not me. I always wanted to work. So when Mom told me I could be a Therapy Dog, I was really happy.

Therapy Dogs help people who need extra love. Mom said we would learn to help people together and that made me feel very special.

Mom also said there would be a lot to learn, but that she would teach me. I like learning new things. Mom teaches me a lot, but the most important lesson is to *'Pay attention!'*

Mom gave me a very pretty collar and leash. When I wear these I know we are going to *'work.'* During our visits, people take me for walks, brush my fur, and hug me a lot. They give me yummy treats too. But my favorite part of working is making people happy. Soon I became known as *Coco the Love Dog*.

I love it when Mom says, *'Let's go to work.'* "

Now, you too can enjoy a visit from Coco the Love Dog by reading her very special book. Read *Coco the Love Dog* to experience the power of her *"doggy love."*

Who will twirl on
her tippy toes with you?

Coco the Love Dog

Who will give you kisses?

Coco the Love Dog

Who will cuddle and snuggle with you?

Coco the Love Dog

Who will sneak treats with you?

Coco the Love Dog

Who will let you tickle her belly?

Coco the Love Dog

Who will read stories with you?

Coco the Love Dog

Who will share secrets
with you?

Coco the Love Dog

Who will play with you when you're lonely?

Coco the Love Dog

Who will make you smile
when you're sad?

Coco the Love Dog

Who will be your friend forever?

Coco the Love Dog

Who will love you always?

Coco the Love Dog

Sue Grundfest

Photo by Vidura Barrios

Author, Sue Grundfest combined her lifelong love for animals and volunteer work to found Love Dog Adventures LLC, a leading supplier of books and toys for children, including the book *Coco the Love Dog*. Coco, Sue's miniature poodle, is the main inspiration for the venture.

Ms. Grundfest has been working with Coco for eight years now as a certified pet therapy pair. They enjoy making visits to charitable organizations throughout the New York Metropolitan area like Rivington House, New Alternatives for Children (NAC), Lighthouse International, Coalition for the Homeless, and Bide-A-Wee to name just a few.

In addition to her work with Love Dog Adventures LLC, Sue is vice president at a global cosmetics company based in New York City where she has enjoyed working for the past twenty-one years. She considers having started the company's corporate volunteer program her proudest professional achievement.

Currently Sue resides on the Upper East Side in Manhattan with Coco.

Daniel J. Mahoney

Illustrator, Daniel J. Mahoney is a self-taught artist who has written and illustrated *The Saturday Escape*, *The Perfect Clubhouse*, and *A Really Good Snowman* for Clarion Books, which was chosen by The Society of Illustrators for their 2005 The Original Art Show. Daniel's artwork has also graced the pages of educational literature for young people, including contributions to publications by Scholastic, Scott Foresman, McGraw-Hill, and *Weekly Reader* magazine. Daniel was born and raised in Albany, New York, where he currently resides with his wife Jean and their son Ryan.

For more information about
Therapy Dogs and the friends
Coco works with, visit:

www.bideawee.org
www.nac-inc.org
www.lighthouse.org
www.vcny.org
www.coalitionforthehomeless.org
www.deltasociety.org